E 708 049 047 802 39

Blazer

Crime

by David Orme

Ransom

Nottinghamshire County Council Community Services	
PETERS	11-Sep-2008
364	£4.99

Trailblazers
Crime

by David Orme
Educational consultant: Helen Bird

Illustrated by Øivind Hovland

Published by Ransom Publishing Ltd.
51 Southgate Street, Winchester, Hampshire SO23 9EH
www.ransom.co.uk

ISBN   978 184167 651 7

First published in 2008

Copyright © 2008 Ransom Publishing Ltd.

Illustrations copyright © 2008 Øivind Hovland
'Get the Facts' section - images copyright: people smuggling courtsey Ansar Burney Trust; antivirus shields - cyrop; binary code - Alexey Khlobystov; goat - Eric Isselée; bonfire - Andy Heyward; fingerprint - Dean Turner; CCTV camera - Rudi Tapper; crime scene - Christine Glade; graveyard - Diane Diederich; pirate flag - Dawn Hudson; DNA - Kirsty Pargeter; black hand letter, computer virus, feet - illustrated by Neil Smith, copyright Ransom Publishing Ltd.; handcuffed man - Johannes Norpoth; Mafia boss - Matjaz Boncina.

Every effort has been made to locate all copyright holders of material used in this book. If any errors or omissions have occurred, corrections will be made in future editions of this book.

A CIP catalogue record of this book is available from the British Library.

The rights of David Orme to be identified as the author and of Øivind Hovland to be identified as the illustrator of this Work have been asserted by them in accordance with sections 77 and 78 of the Copyright, Design and Patents Act 1988.

Crime

Contents

Crime

Get the facts

Piracy and body snatching

Pirates

Were all pirates really tough men?

No. One of the most famous pirates was a woman, called **Anne Bonny**. She was born around 1700.

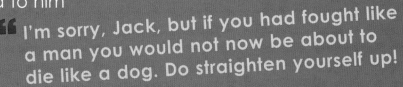

Anne Bonny

At 16, she ran away and married a pirate. When she grew tired of him, she ran off to sea with another pirate called Jack. She dressed as a man, and was so good with pistols and cutlass that no one guessed she was a woman.

She wasn't the only woman on board. Another pirate, called **Mary Read**, was just as fierce. Once, the pirate ship was attacked. All the men were drunk – so Anne and Mary had to defend the ship themselves!

When the pirates were captured the punishment was hanging. Anne pretended to be pregnant, so she wasn't hanged. Jack was.

Anne said to him

> I'm sorry, Jack, but if you had fought like a man you would not now be about to die like a dog. Do straighten yourself up!

Body snatchers

Between 1700 and 1830 many bodies were stolen by thieves called **body snatchers**. They dug them up from **churchyards**.

They bought bodies from people who ran hospitals and workhouses.

Some criminals didn't wait until the person was dead. They murdered them and sold the body.

Why would anyone want a dead body?

The body snatchers sold them to doctors. They used the bodies to teach **anatomy** (the study of the human body). They used them to practise operations.

Body snatching only stopped in **1832**, when new laws allowed doctors to use unclaimed bodies for anatomy.

In fact, stealing a body wasn't a serious crime. The law said that a body didn't belong to anyone.

Stealing anything buried with the body, such as clothes, **was** a serious crime. The punishment was hanging.

Gangs and gangsters

The Mafia

Who are the Mafia?

The Mafia began as a secret society on the island of **Sicily**.

During the 20th century, many people from Sicily went to live in America. Mafia families began organising crime in big cities such as **New York** and **Chicago**.

Some of these criminals were members of **Black Hand** gangs. These gangs sent people letters demanding money. There was a black handprint on the letter. If you didn't pay up you were in trouble.

Mafia terms

The Mob – *the Mafia*

The Boss (sometimes called the **Godfather** or the **Don**) – *head of a Mafia family*

The Underboss – *second in command*

In 1920 alcohol was banned in the United States. The Mafia smuggled alcohol into the U.S. from other countries. They set up secret bars called **speakeasies**, where people went to drink.

The ban ended in 1933.

The Mafia turned to other crimes such as murder, supplying drugs and gambling.

Who was Al Capone?

Al Capone, called **Scarface**, became head of the Chicago Mafia in 1925.

He ran speakeasies and gambling houses. Anyone who stood up to Capone ended up in hospital or dead! Even the local police and Mayor were afraid of him.

In 1929, seven members of a rival mob were machine-gunned on Capone's orders – but Capone was out of town at the time!

Capone spent seven years in prison for not paying tax – but he was never convicted of murder.

Modern crime

As the world changes, some crimes disappear and new ones take their place.

A lot of modern crime is connected with **drugs**. Drugs like heroin and cocaine were not made illegal until 1924. Before then, they were used in everyday medicine you could buy from the local chemist.

Smuggling, making and selling illegal drugs is done by gangs, just like the gangs that smuggled alcohol in to America in the 1920s.

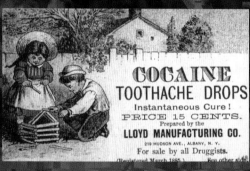

Cocaine toothache drops.

Mrs Winslow's Soothing Syrup for your baby – it contained a type of heroin.

Drug-taking causes a lot of crime. Because people become addicted to drugs, they often steal to get money to buy them.

Drugs also affect people's behaviour. People on drugs may become violent.

People smuggling

There are many reasons why people want to move to another country. They may be badly treated by the government or by other people in their own country. Or they may be looking for a better life.

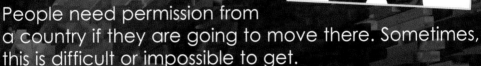

People need permission from a country if they are going to move there. Sometimes, this is difficult or impossible to get.

People smugglers are criminals who charge people money to smuggle them into a country.

Sometimes they are smuggled in the back of trucks. Many people have died through lack of air.

Chinese people-smuggling gangs are called **Snakeheads**. They try and smuggle people into western Europe and the U.S.A.

People for sale in Canada?
THE ANSWER WILL SHOCK YOU.

Every year, people like Sonia are deceived or forced into a life no one would choose – sold into the sex trade, locked up in sweatshops, made to work for little or no pay. They are victims of human trafficking.

HUMAN TRAFFICKING IS A SERIOUS CRIME.
www.justice.gc.ca

Government of Canada   Gouvernement du Canada   Canada

11

Internet crime

Criminals can use the Internet to get hold of your money.

It is difficult to catch these criminals. They can work from any country. It is not always easy to find out where they really are.

Scams

You need to be careful when buying things on the Internet. What's on offer might sound real, but you could end up with

- **fake** watches and CDs
- **fake** medical drugs
- **nothing at all** – they might just keep your money!

Internet criminals want information about you –

- details of your **bank accounts**
- the **passwords** you use when you are online
- the numbers on your **credit cards**.

12

How do they do this?

They might send you an email that looks as if it comes from your bank. It will ask you to remind them what your bank details are. This is called **phishing**.

Would you fall for this? *Lots of people do!*

Viruses

Viruses can do bad things to your computer. It may stop working properly, or you could lose all your important information.

Make sure your computer is protected against viruses!

Why do people send out viruses?

Sometimes people just like causing other people problems, but sometimes the viruses can be involved in crime.

- A virus can make your computer send out emails. You may not know that this is happening. These emails can pass on scams.

- The virus could 'read' what you are typing into your computer and send it to someone else. This is another way for internet criminals to get hold of your bank details.

13

Punishing crime in history

In the past, punishments for crime were very severe. Being caught often meant the death penalty. This is called **capital punishment**.

Burning at the stake was once used for serious or religious crimes.

In Britain, burning wasn't abolished until 1790, though for around fifty years before that victims were hung or strangled first.

In the seventeenth and eighteenth century burning was the punishment for **treason** (a serious crime against your country) but only women were burnt – men got away with hanging!

The last person to be burnt at the stake was Catherine Murphy in 1789. She had been hanged first.

Hanging was the most common form of punishment. In the eighteenth century there were 222 crimes you could be hanged for, including damaging London Bridge!

The last hangings in Britain took place in 1964.

Transportation was introduced in the seventeenth century as an alternative to capital punishment.

People were taken to countries such as America and Australia, where they had to work without being paid.

Most of them never returned.

Transportation was abolished in 1868.

> ### DORSET
> ANY PERSON WILFULLY INJURING
> ANY PART OF THIS COUNTY BRIDGE
> WILL BE GUILTY OF FELONY AND
> UPON CONVICTION LIABLE TO BE
> ### TRANSPORTED FOR LIFE
> BY THE COURT
> T FOOKS

SILLY PUNISHMENTS

Tickle torture

In ancient Rome, people were tied down and their bare feet were covered with salt. Goats would then be made to lick the salt off!

Solving crime

The police use modern technology to fight crime.

Fingerprints

In the nineteenth century, scientists discovered two important facts about fingerprints.

1 Everyone has a different fingerprint pattern.

2 Your fingerprint pattern stays the same for your whole life.

The method of using fingerprints to solve crime was developed in India. It was first used in Britain in 1901, and in the USA in 1902.

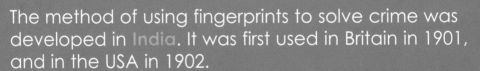

DNA

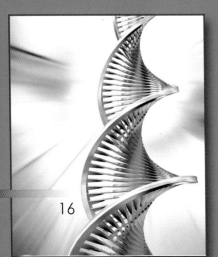

Some people say that DNA is a modern version of fingerprints.

Our DNA is the pattern our cells use to build our bodies. Everyone's DNA is different.

16

If a criminal leaves something as tiny as a hair from their head, or a spot of blood, it can be used to check their DNA.

Some people say everyone's DNA should be kept on file. Other people say this is wrong.

WHAT DO YOU THINK?

CCTV

CCTV (Closed Circuit TeleVision) is used to check for traffic problems and for street crime.

If you walk around a town, you could be on camera up to 300 times in a day!

Many crimes have been solved with the help of CCTV, and police have been able to sort out fights and other trouble before it gets out of hand.

Some people say it is wrong. People should be free to go about their lives without being watched all the time.

WHAT DO YOU THINK?

Trail
Blazers

Burke
and
Hare

Chapter 1:
Edinburgh, Scotland, 1827

"Curse the man! He owed me four pounds! How can I get my money back, now he's dead?"

William Hare was an angry man. He ran a cheap lodging house in Edinburgh. An old man who stayed there had died owing the rent.

Hare's friend William Burke lived in the same house. He was an old friend of Hare's.

"You can't get money from a dead man, Bill, that's for sure."

But Hare had an idea.

A few days later, in a hospital on the other side of the city a doctor called Robert Knox was getting ready to teach his students.

Professor Knox taught anatomy. But he had a problem. He needed dead bodies to cut up – and they were very difficult to find.

There was a knock at his door. It was Burke and Hare – and they had a body for sale!

Burke and Hare got seven pounds for the body of the old man. They had put a sack of wood in his coffin instead of a body!

Chapter 2:
A great way to make money

Burke and Hare thought this was a great way to make money.

"The problem is, Bill, we'll have to wait until someone else dies," said Burke.

But William Hare was not a patient man.

A lodger called Joe was sick. He was the next victim. They got him drunk on whisky then suffocated him. That night, they took his body to the professor.

By February 1828 Burke and Hare were short of money again. They invited an old lady called Abigail Simpson into the house. They got her drunk and suffocated her.

Professor Knox was really pleased to get her body, because it was so fresh! He paid Burke and Hare fifteen pounds for Abigail. He didn't ask them how they got the body.

Chapter 3:
A big mistake

By the middle of 1828 Burke and Hare had murdered fourteen people and sold their bodies to Professor Knox.

Then they made a big mistake.

Their next victim was called Daft Jamie. He wandered round the streets of Edinburgh. Everybody knew Jamie.

He was a young victim and he put up a fight. But Burke and Hare managed to kill him.

By the middle of 1828, Burke and Hare had murdered 14 people. Then they decided to kill a young man called Daft Jamie. He was young and put up a fight ...

Selling Jamie's body was a big mistake ...

The next morning there was a huge fuss at the anatomy class. Some of Professor Knox's students recognised Daft Jamie!

The professor told them they were wrong. It wasn't Jamie at all. But just to make sure no one could recognise him, he cut up Jamie's face first!

Chapter 4:
Guilty or not guilty?

Burke and Hare were getting careless. In November 1828 they murdered Mary Docherty. They hid her body under the bed, but other people who lived in the house found it. They called the police.

William Burke was hanged for his crimes in January 1829, but because Hare had given evidence against Burke he was let off. No one knows what happened to him.

Many people thought Professor Knox was just as guilty. A mob attacked his house and smashed his windows, but he was not punished. He carried on as a doctor.

This rhyme was popular in Edinburgh at the time:

Up the close and down the stair,

In the house with Burke and Hare.

Burke's the butcher, Hare's the thief,

Knox, the boy who buys the beef.

Crime word check

alcohol	murder
anatomy	operations
bank account	phishing
behaviour	pirate
body snatcher	punishment
CCTV	scam
churchyard	smuggling
cocaine	Snakeheads
convicted	strangled
credit card	speakeasy
cutlass	suffocated
DNA	transportation
fingerprint	victim
gambling	violent
heroin	virus
Internet	workhouse
lodging house	
Mafia	